To my grandson, Max
—J.S.

To my sister, Aggles,
with love
—L.D.

10 Trim-the-Tree'ers

a holiday counting book

by **Janet Schulman** • illustrated by **Linda Davick**

Alfred A. Knopf

New York

10 little neighbors
about to trim their tree.
They'll dress for the occasion.

R0425121964

Turn the page and see!

1 shiny golden star
at the very tip-top.

2 strings of flashing lights
that just won't stop.

3 little angels with halos
and with wings.

4 Santa's elves making toys that he brings.

5 swift reindeer—they know how to fly.

6 lacy snowflakes
that fall from the sky.

7 jolly men all made of snow.

8 candy canes—no eating them, though!

9 menorah candles to mark the gift of light.

10 pretty presents to make our holiday bright.

10 trim-the-tree'ers,
now their job is done.
It's time to serenade
their pets and everyone.

We wish you a merry Christmas,
We wish you a merry Christmas,
We wish you a merry Christmas,
And a happy New Year.

THIS IS A BORZOI BOOK PUBLISHED BY ALFRED A. KNOPF

Text copyright © 2010 by Janet Schulman
Illustrations copyright © 2010 by Linda Davick

Visit us on the Web! www.randomhouse.com/kids

Educators and librarians, for a variety of teaching tools, visit us at www.randomhouse.com/teachers

Library of Congress Cataloging-in-Publication Data
Schulman, Janet.
10 trim-the-tree'ers : a holiday counting book / by Janet Schulman ; illustrated by Linda Davick. — 1st ed.
p. cm.
Summary: Ten young neighbors wear costumes as they decorate a Christmas tree with different items,
from one shiny star on top to ten wrapped gifts below.
ISBN 978-0-375-86658-6 (trade) — ISBN 978-0-375-96658-3 (lib. bdg.)
[1. Stories in rhyme. 2. Christmas—Fiction. 3. Counting.] I. Davick, Linda, ill. II. Title. III. Title: Ten trim-the-tree'ers.
PZ8.3.S29737Aag 2010   [E]—dc22   2009017496

MANUFACTURED IN CHINA
September 2010   10 9 8 7 6 5 4 3 2 1   First Edition
Random House Children's Books supports the First Amendment and celebrates the right to read.